Contents

Red Bananas

Dragon Hills

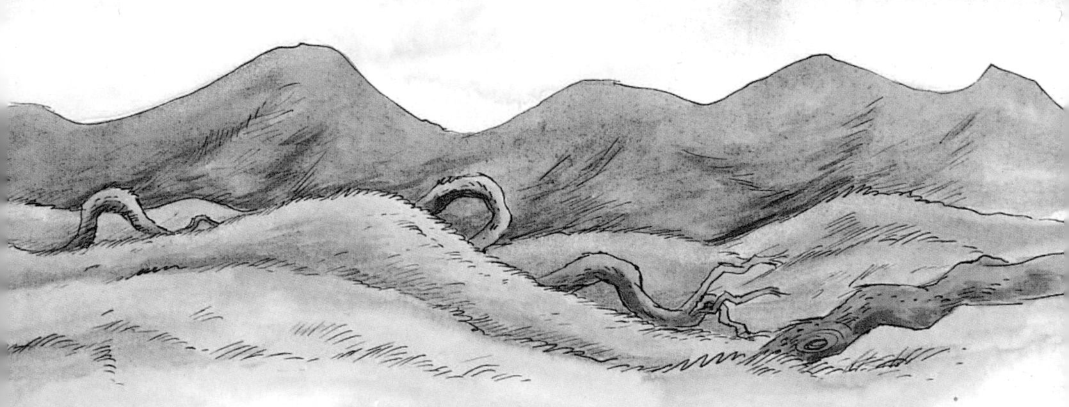

Lily licked the mixing spoon like a large lollipop. She asked, 'Gran, why do they laugh at Granda sometimes?'

'Who laughs at your granda, my lovely?'

'People. They say he's strange.'

'Well, he is different from the rest, Lily,' said Gran. 'That's why I married him.'

Gran pushed the cake tin into the oven, shut the door, then wiped floury hands on her apron. 'Your granda would rather talk to the hills than to people and that upsets folks. But there's good reason his being the way he is. Now you go and find Granda, Lily. Bring him home for a slice of cake.'

So Lily went out into the garden, through the gate and up the path to the hills. She found Granda sitting on a hump, whistling to himself.

There's cake in the oven, Granda.'

'My favourite?'

'Your ginger special,' smiled Lily, sitting close to Granda and leaning against his warmth.

'Granda, why do you like the hills so much?'

He smiled. 'Because these are Dragon Hills.'

'Real dragons?' asked Lily.

'Real sleeping dragons,' said Granda. 'Would you like to hear how I came to know all about them?'

'Yes, please,' said Lily.

'Well,' said Granda, 'in years long gone, the people of our village were terribly scared of the dragons that lived around here.'

'Then why did they live near them?' asked Lily.

'Because they needed something that the dragons had.'

'What was that?'

'They needed fire,' said Granda, 'and they planned to steal it from the dragons' fiery breath. You see, the villagers needed to warm their homes, and cook their food, and make life good. So they chose the biggest, bravest man in the village. They gave him a fine spear and they called him Fire Snatcher. My da, your great-granda, Lily, was Fire Snatcher and hero of the village.'

'But how did he snatch the fire?' asked Lily.

Fire Snatcher

'Well, Lily, dragons are strange creatures,' said Granda. 'They lay their eggs, then sleep for a full ninety years until the eggs are ready to hatch. When that happens, the dragon mothers wake up to care for their babies.

'It takes ten years to grow the baby dragons up. Then once they are grown, the mothers lay more eggs and settle down again to sleep.

'The dragons were in their sleep-years when my da was Fire Snatcher. All he had to do was creep, tiptoe-quiet into the hills, then jump, sudden, on a sleeping dragon and poke it with his spear.

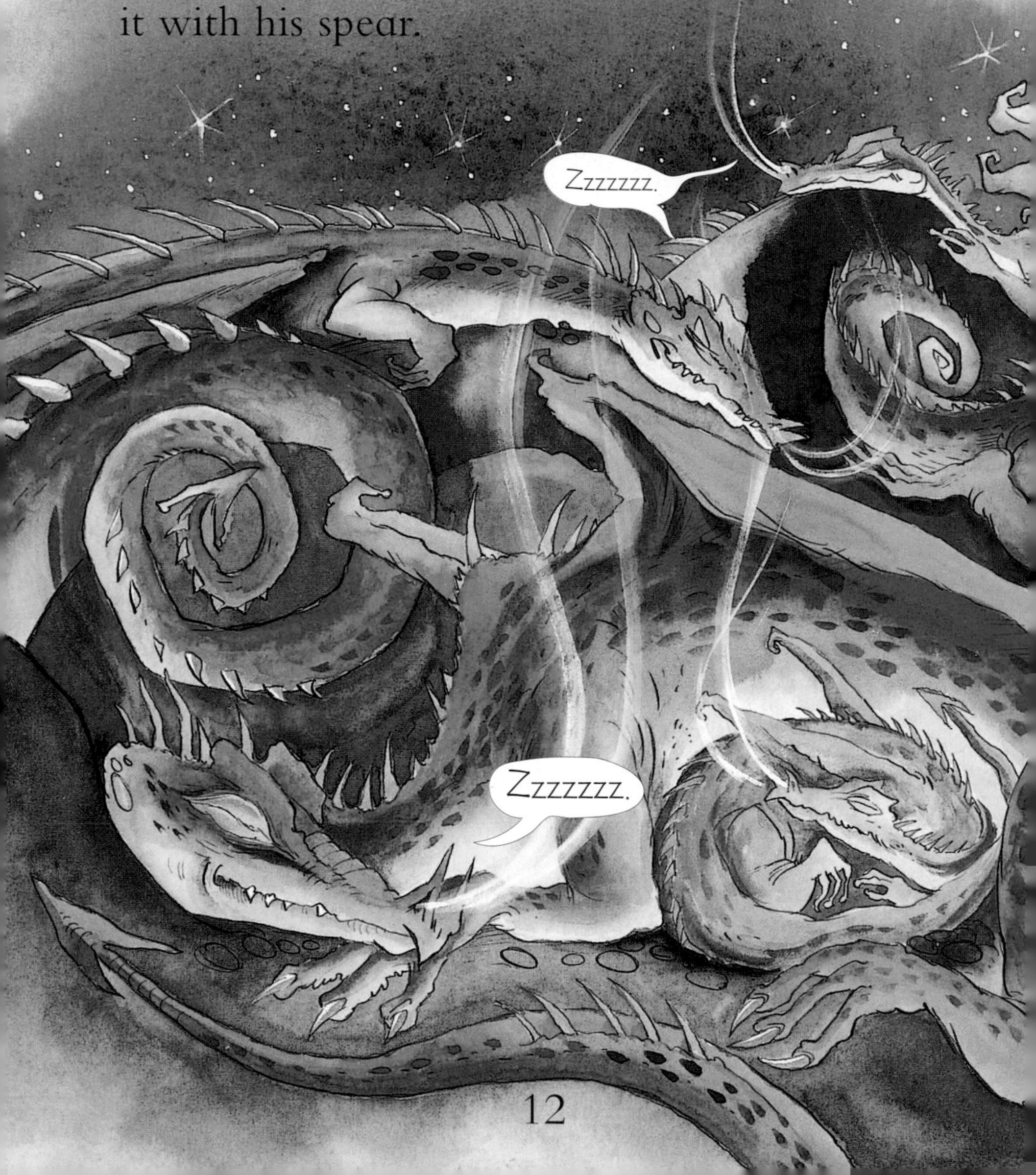

'The poor beast would start from its sleep and blaze with fright, just as you or I would if anybody jabbed at us with a needle while we were sleeping. But it worked. It made the dragon roar fire.

‘As it roared, the Fire Snatcher thrust his torch of dry wood into the flare of the dragon’s fiery breath to light it.

‘Then he’d run home as fast as a man could with his blazing torch – the villagers cheering him all the way.

'Fire's a strange and generous thing, you know. Take all you want from it and it'll still be there. Once the Fire Snatcher had got his flame, there was always plenty of fire to share. For weeks, months, years after, there'd be warmth and light.

'The Fire Snatcher would keep watch, making sure that there was always a fire alight somewhere in the village.'

'But what happened to the dragon who'd been spiked by the spear?' asked Lily.

Granda shrugged. 'Poor beast would be all heart-a-thumping for a time, I dare say. She'd lick her wound. In time she'd go back to sleep, but she wouldn't sleep easy. Frights like that live long after the reason for them is done with.

'And it was on account of that uneasy sleep that I came to hear another story about the dragons.'

'Oh, please tell it to me!' begged Lily.

'All right then,' laughed Granda.

Fire!

'One hot, humid summer's night, the people of the village were asleep. The dragons slept too, a slump of slumbering hills that rumbled every now and again with thundering snores.

'The Dragon Hills were still as stone – a gentle breeze coming from their sleeping breaths. A tiny puff of thistledown came floating on that breeze. It breathed up and down above the great beasts until, all of a sudden, it was breathed right up into the nose of a dragon – the last one to have been spiked by the Fire Snatcher.

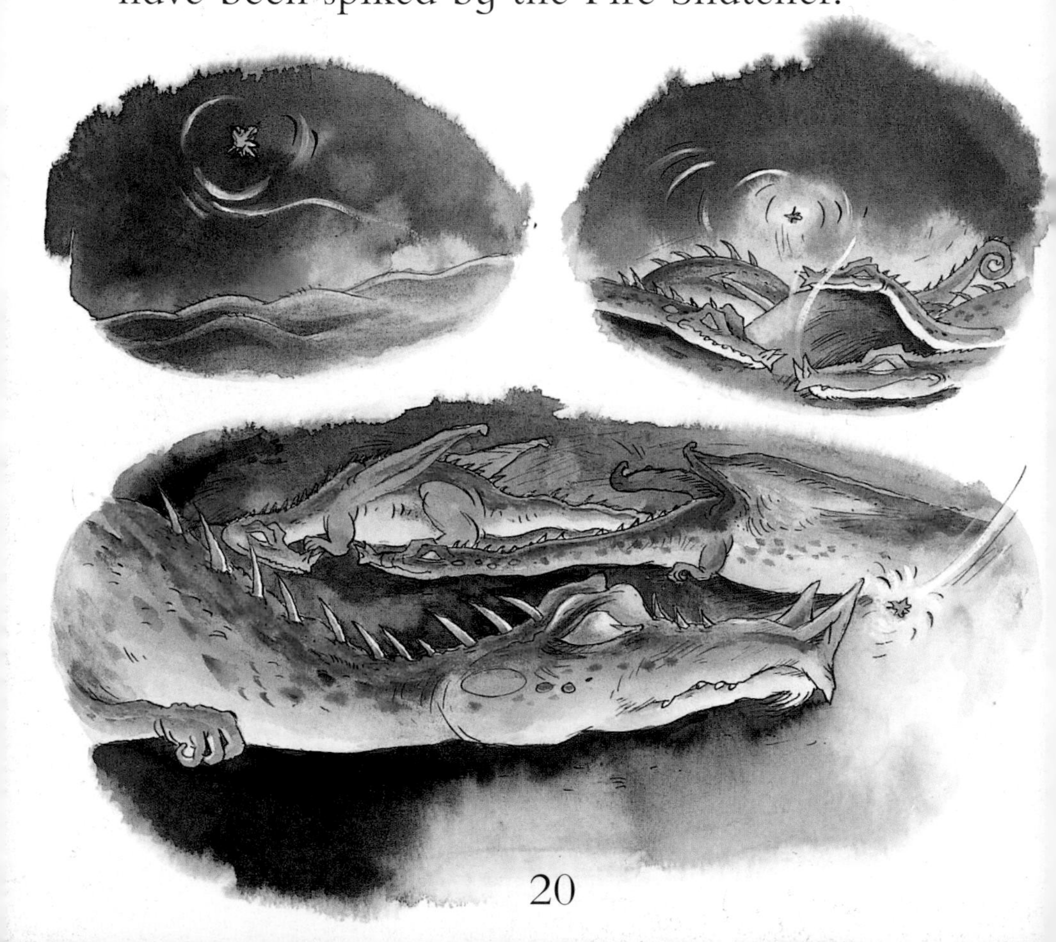

'She was only a young dragon, and she'd been made jumpy-frit by the scare of it all.

The thistledown tickled her nose and made her wake with a sneezy snort.

‘A tiny spark from her firey breath drifted onto the breeze and floated over to the village where it fell down, down onto a pile of hay and burst into flames. Fire spread, quick fast. Fire’s a greedy beast as well as a generous one, Lily. It wanted more than hay.

It leapt and licked and lapped its way up the village, house by house, street by street, burning everything.

Babies

'The people woke and smelled smoke, and saw and heard the red roaring fire. They snatched their children from their beds and bundled up their belongings. They ran from their burning village, up into the cool darkness of the Dragon Hills.

'The commotion of it all made the dragons stir. The hills humped and bumped so that the people stumbled and tumbled and dropped their bundles in the smoky dark. They picked up their things and each other as best they could and ran on and away.'

'I'd have run too, if the hills had moved under me!' said Lily. 'What happened then?'

'Well, it so happened that the morning after the fire, the dragons began to wake from their long sleep. They woke, bleary-blinking and yawning in the bright morning light, just as their eggs were hatching.

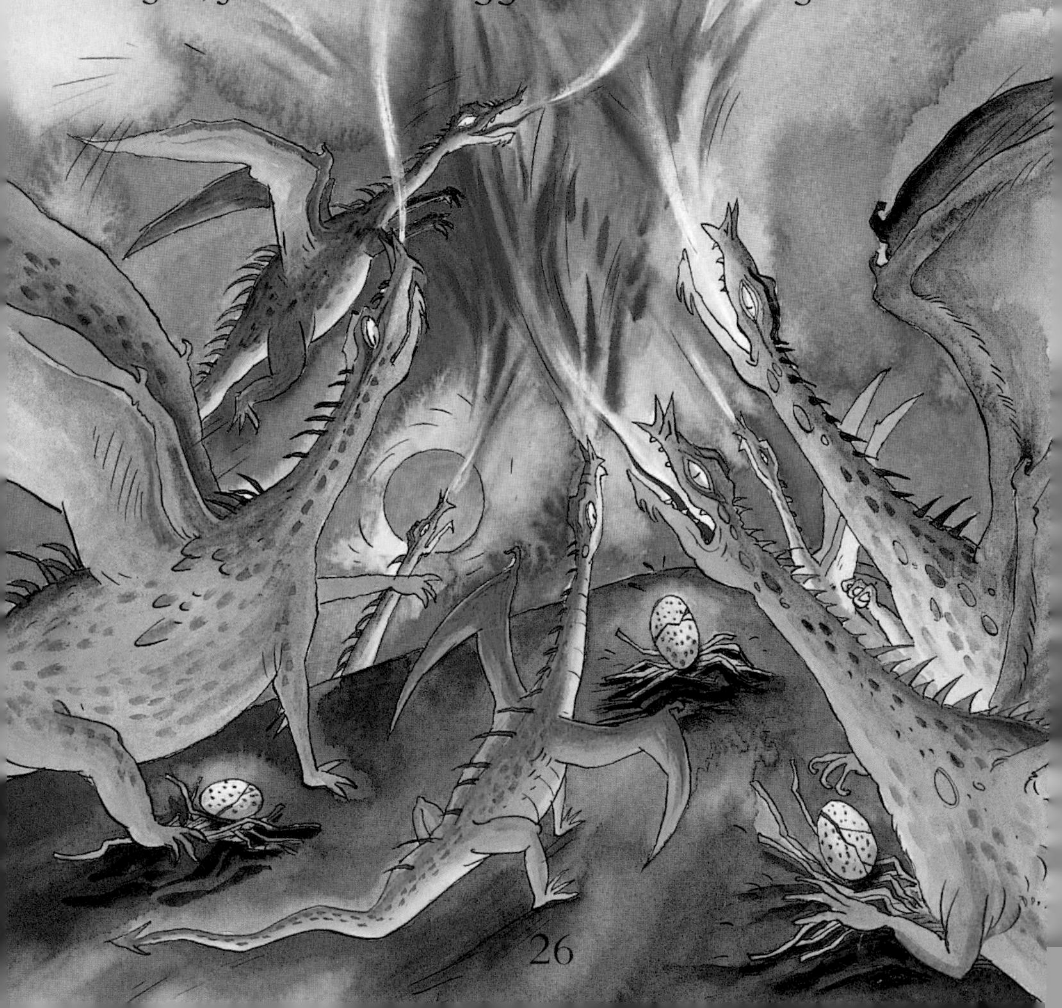

‘But one mother missed seeing her egg hatch. She had woken to find its shell already broken into pieces. And lying by the bits was not just one baby, but two!

‘Goodness! thought the dragon mother. Twins!

‘But you never saw twins less like each other than those two babies were.

‘One baby was very like the other baby dragons. She was green and scaly and glinted in the sunshine.

‘“So pretty!” sang the dragon mother.

‘The other baby was pink and soft and bald, except for a fluff of black fur on the top of his head.

‘What an odd little one he is, she thought.

'But when the odd baby began to cry, the dragon mother cradled him in the scoop of her wing, and soothed him and rocked him as any mother would.

'The other dragon mothers moved away and whispered when they saw the strange baby. But the baby's mother told him, "Don't you worry, my funny chick. I love you."

'She hummed a dragon lullaby and rocked him to sleep, and put him curled alongside his dragon sister, and he was happy.

'The dragon mother looked after both her babies for almost ten years. One grew into a beautiful dragoness, the other into an ordinary human boy. The boy loved his dragon sister and she loved him, but he wished that he was more like her and their dragon friends.

'So he made himself a covering of green leaves that looked like scales, and he learnt to sing dragon songs with the others. They called him Dragon Boy.'

'So, was he really like a dragon?' asked Lily.

'In many ways he was,' said Granda. 'But he still felt as if he was the odd one out.

'As the sun began to set, Dragon Boy turned for home. But he was still so cross that he kicked angrily at the flint stones under his feet. As one stone struck another, Dragon Boy saw a flash of yellow.

'He kicked the stones again, harder this time, and saw a spark flash in the growing dark.

"Fire!" shouted Dragon Boy. "I've made fire without having to breathe it!"

'Quickly he began collecting dry grass and sticks and bigger logs. Then, crouching down with his back to the wind to shelter any spark, he struck two sharp flints, one against another. CLACK! At first the stones just smelled a little smoky.

'CLACK, CLACK, CLACK. He struck them again and again, until at last a spark flashed and took to the grass. As the grass smouldered and smoked, Dragon Boy blew on it gently. He sang it a fiery dragon song, and suddenly the smouldering flowered into flames.'

'Real fire?' asked Lily.

'Real fire,' said Granda.

'Dragon Boy added stick after stick and log after log and built his fire into something so powerful big that it lit and warmed the night all around. He hoped that the dragons would see the faraway fire and know that it was his.'

'Did they?' asked Lily.

'They did,' said Granda with a smile.

'But people from the village saw it too.

You see, they'd come back and rebuilt their homes soon after they'd burnt down. But they lived without fire now. Even the Fire Snatcher didn't dare try to steal fire from the dragons he could see awake in the hills. So the villagers lived in cold, damp and dark homes.'

Who's that?
Is it a boy?
He's wearing leaves!

'They must have been excited when they saw Dragon Boy's bonfire!' said Lily.

'Oh, they were,' said Granda. 'They came hurrying up the mountain, cheering and dancing. Dragon Boy was scared when he saw them all running at him. But when the people saw the boy in his green leaf suit, looking wild, they were the ones that stopped still!

'All except for one woman. She ran straight to Dragon Boy with her arms and smile wide, wide.'

'Dragon Boy's ma!' cried Lily. 'I bet it was Dragon Boy's ma!'

'You're right, my love,' said Granda. 'It was Dragon Boy's human ma who'd dropped and lost him all those years before. She knew him straight away. She told the people, "Look! See! It's the Fire Snatcher's son. It's the baby I lost. He's come home, bringing us fire!"

Dragon Granda

'The villagers made a hero of the boy then,' said Granda. 'They liked him for bringing them fire. But it's a strange thing to be a hero when you're used to being the one who's no good. Dragon Boy felt quite sad.

'He went back to living with his human ma and da, and the brothers and sisters he'd never met before. He missed his dragon ma and sister, of course. But the dragons had laid more eggs by then and were going to sleep, so he'd have been all alone if he'd stayed in the hills.'

'Did he ever visit the dragons?' asked Lily.

'Oh, yes,' said Granda. 'Every day he'd come up here to be with them. Dragon Boy would sit for hours and sing them lullabies.'

Granda sang softly to Lily now,

Hushaby, my darling
Curl snug around to hug around
Your sleepy sleepy sleepy sleepy sleep
While I keep watch and wait for you to wake

'Dragon Boy cried, you know,' said Granda, 'even though he was a big lad.'

'I would have cried too,' said Lily.

'People thought the boy was odd for singing to the hills,' said Granda. 'All except for his ma. She listened when he told her how it was.'

Hushaby, my darling
Curl snug around to hug around
Your sleepy sleepy sleepy sleepy sleep
While I keep watch and wait for you to wake

Granda's old voice wobbled as he sang.

Lily took his big hand in hers and asked him gently, 'Dragon Boy was you, wasn't he?'

Granda smiled. 'He was. He is. And I still sing to my dragon family.'

'Will you teach me your dragon songs?' said Lily. 'Then I can sing to them too.'

'People will likely think that you're as odd as me for singing to the hills.'

'I don't care,' said Lily. 'I'll be different, like you are, Granda.'

Granda got stiffly to his feet, pulling Lily up beside him. 'Well, my little chick, you can begin to understand what it is like to be a dragon by eating a piece of your gran's ginger cake. She adds chilli to the mix, you know, to make it taste of fire.'

'Then I want a big slice, please,' said Lily.